Schoolies™

The Birthday Party

Based on the characters created by
Ellen Crimi-Trent

priddy books

Zippy woke with a happy thought.

He tumbled out of bed, scurried down the stairs and threw open the front door. It was still dark. The sun wasn't up yet.

Whistling happily, Zippy started to get everything ready for his party. First, he put up the decorations.
I hope they won't fall down.

Zippy's sister helped him with the balloons.

Zippy put up the Pin the Tail on the Donkey
and arranged the musical chairs.

He put out cups, cookies, plates and lemonade. Finally, he brought out a special racing car cake!

Zippy looked around the
room to check he hadn't
forgotten anything.

Everything looked super. All that was left was to wait for his friends to arrive.

Zippy watched the clock.
After a while, he began to worry.

He wondered if his friends would think musical chairs was boring.

He wondered if they'd think a racing car cake was silly.

Finally the time came
for the guests to arrive.

Zippy raced to the front door
but nobody was there.

Zippy went back inside the house feeling a little sad and confused.
Maybe I forgot to do something?
Balloons ✓
Car cake ✓
Party Games ✓
Musical chairs ✓

He'd remembered the cookies and lemonade.
He'd remembered to put up the decorations.
He'd remembered everything except...

Zippy felt very silly.

Just then, Zippy heard a noise from the garden. He scooted to the back door.

There in the garden were all of Zippy's friends! When Zippy stepped out of the door, the Schoolies all began to sing.

Zippy could hardly believe his eyes and ears.
Happy birthday to you!
+1
1
=2
We have gifts for you.

The Schoolies piled presents
onto the picnic table.

Zippy told everyone that he had forgotten to send invitations to his party.

The Schoolies all smiled and told him they wouldn't have missed his birthday for anything in the world.

How about some racing games?

They loved the party and all the games that Zippy had planned.